Mr Bear's PICNIC

Debi Gliori

ORCHARD BOOKS

With grateful thanks for
the thousand small kindnesses
shown to me by everyone working on Ward 49
of Simpson's Maternity Pavilion
through the summer of 1994.

This book is dedicated to
all of you with my love.

ORCHARD BOOKS
338 Euston Road, London NW1 3BH
Orchard Books Australia
Level 17/207 Kent Street, Sydney, NSW 2000

First published in 1995 by Orchard Books
First published in paperback in 1996
This edition published in 2008 for Index Books Ltd

ISBN: 978 1 84362 844 6

A CIP catalogue record for this book is available from the British Library.

Printed in China

1 3 5 7 9 10 8 6 4 2

Orchard Books is a division of Hachette Children's Books,
an Hachette Livre UK company.
www.hachettelivre.co.uk

"What a beautiful day!" thought Mr Bear.
"Perfect weather for a picnic."
Mrs Bear snored quietly.

"I'm going to take the baby out for the day," said Mr Bear.
Mrs Bear opened one bleary eye.

"Mmm, that's a good idea," she
yawned. "I'm sure the Grizzle-Bears
would like to come too – they love picnics,"
and she turned over and went back to sleep.

Mr Bear and the baby stopped at the
Grizzle-Bears' house. There was nobody there.
"Thank heavens," said Mr Bear. "They must
have gone out for the day. Now we can have
a peaceful picnic on our own."
Just then they heard a voice from high
in the treetops.

"Here we are, Mr Bear," said Fred.
"Did you say 'picnic'?" said Ted.
"Can we come too?" said Fuzz. Mr Bear groaned.
"Please?" begged Fred, Ted and Fuzz,
tumbling down from the tree in a furry heap
and running off to say goodbye to their mother.

It took ages to find the right picnic spot.

First Mr Bear led them to
his favourite meadow.
"Dad *always* brings us here,"
moaned Fred. "It's *boring*."

So Mr Bear took them
further afield.
"This is a fly-infested
swamp," said Ted.

With a sigh Mr Bear led
them deeper into the woods.
"This gives me the creeps,"
said Fuzz.

At last they came to the perfect place. Baby Bear found a grassy hollow and Mr Bear stretched out in the sun for a snooze.

"I'm starving," said Fred, bouncing
on Mr Bear's tummy. "I could eat six lunches."

"I'm ravenous," said Ted. "I could eat six lunches
and whatever's in that basket."

"I'm famished," said Fuzz. "I could eat six lunches,
whatever's in that basket *and* the basket as well."

Mr Bear stood up with a sigh.
"Anything for peace," he said, opening the
picnic basket. "Let's see what's for lunch."
Mr Bear pulled out a teddy.
"That's not a very good lunch," said Fred.
"You can't eat toys," said Ted, glaring at Mr Bear.

"You brought the wrong basket," said Fuzz.
The baby began to cry.

"Change of plan," said Mr Bear. "We'll have a fishy picnic," and he strode off to a rock, dipped his paw in the water and waited.

The Grizzle-Bears waited too.

"Maybe I should wiggle my paw like a worm," said Mr Bear. "I know I could catch something, if I just...

s-t-r-e-t-c-h-e-d...

a bit... further."

"HHLLBBBBLUB," said Mr Bear,
slipping head first into the pond.
"Dablublubblub," cried Baby Bear,
clinging on tightly.

"Our Dad never gets wet when he goes fishing," said Fred.

"And he always catches lots of fish," said Ted.

"All you're going to catch is a cold," added Fuzz.

"I don't think we're *ever* going to have a picnic."

"Right – THAT'S IT!" roared Mr Bear.
"Shhh, you'll scare away the fish," said Fred.
"I don't CARE!" yelled Mr Bear.

"Me neither," said Ted. "I don't even like fish."

"They've got jaggy bones…" said Fred.

"And slimy skin…" said Ted.

"And yukky eyeballs," said Fuzz.

"I couldn't agree more," said Mr Bear.

"Come on, I've got a better idea."

The young Grizzle-Bears trailed uphill.
"Nearly there," said Mr Bear. "Look!"
Overhead, tucked in the branches of a
tree, was a golden dome surrounded by
lots of buzzing bees. Mr Bear settled
Baby Bear in the basket, and began
to climb the tree.

Fred, Ted and Fuzz watched as
Mr Bear gently dipped his paw
into the buzzing dome.

"You're really good at that,"
said Fred.

"When our Dad does that,
he gets stung," said Ted.

Mr Bear pulled out a big chunk of honeycomb and climbed back down.

"I love honey," said Fred. "I could eat the whole honeycomb."

"I could eat the whole honeycomb *and* the hive it came from," said Ted.

"I could eat the whole honeycomb, and the hive *and* the bees as well," said Fuzz.

"You must be starving," said Mrs Bear when they arrived home. "You took the wrong basket."

"Yes, but look what we've found!" said Mr Bear.

"Honey!" said Mrs Bear.

"Let's all have a picnic."

"Out of interest," said Mr Bear, "just what did happen to the *other* picnic?"

"Aha," said Mrs Bear. "That's another story…"